PATRICIA POLACCO

Appelemando's Dreams

PHILOMEL BOOKS

New York

Philomel Books, a division of The Putnam & Grosset Group,
200 Madison Avenue, New York, NY 10016. Philomel Books, Reg. U.S. Pat. & Tm. Off.
Sandcastle and the Sandcastle logo are trademarks belonging to The Putnam & Grosset Group.
First Sandcastle edition 1995. Published simultaneously in Canada.
Printed in Hong Kong by South China Printing Co. (1988) Ltd.
The text is set in Sabon. Book design by Nanette Stevenson.
Library of Congress Cataloging-in-Publication Data
Polacco, Patricia. Appelemando's dreams / by Patricia Polacco. p. cm.
Summary: Because he spends his time dreaming, the villagers are
convinced that Appelemando will never amount to much but in time
his dreams change the village and all the people in it.
[1. Dreams—Fiction. 2. Imagination—Fiction.] I. Title.
PZ7.P75186Ap 1991 [E]—dc20 90-19716 CIP AC
ISBN (hardcover) 0-399-21800-9
3 5 7 9 10 8 6 4
ISBN (Sandcastle) 0-399-22835-7
1 3 5 7 9 10 8 6 4 2
First Sandcastle Books Impression

The author is donating a portion of her proceeds toward the restoration of
children's bookstores damaged or destroyed in the great California earthquake of 1989.

For Enzo,
and Valerie Lewis

To the keepers of dreams:
Monica Holmes and Jan Gottlieb at *Hicklebee's Children's Book Emporium*,
Harriet Zander at *Chanticleer Books for the Young*,
Shirley Masengill at *Lane's Books*,
and Fern Skowlund at *Toad Hall Books*.

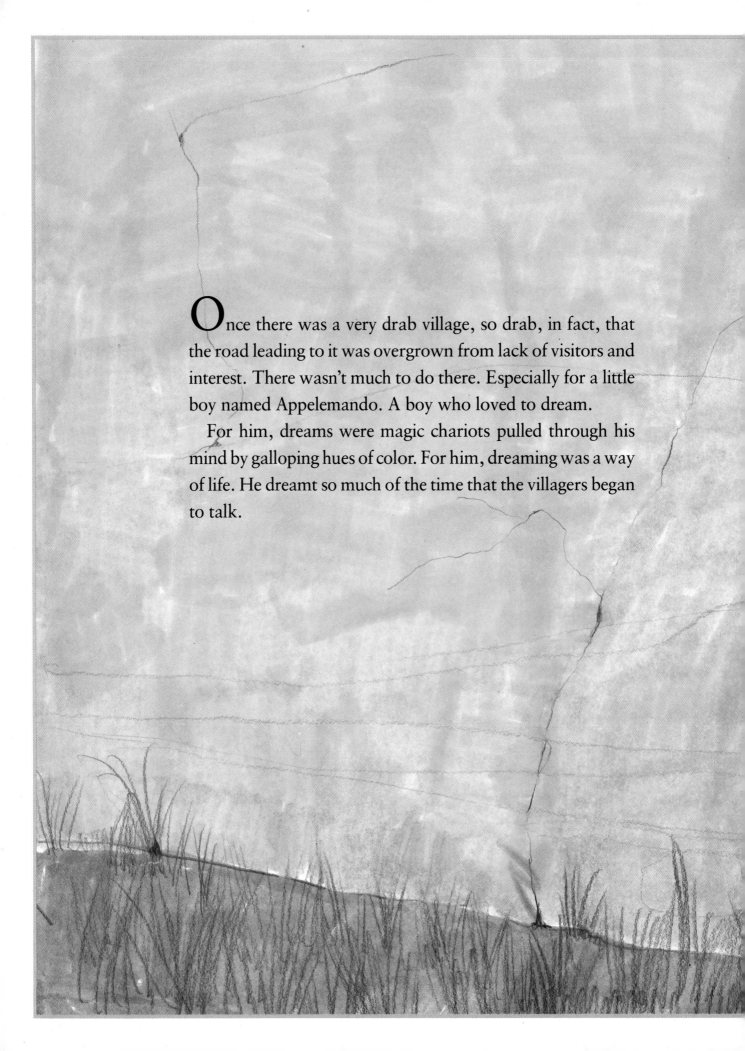

Once there was a very drab village, so drab, in fact, that the road leading to it was overgrown from lack of visitors and interest. There wasn't much to do there. Especially for a little boy named Appelemando. A boy who loved to dream.

For him, dreams were magic chariots pulled through his mind by galloping hues of color. For him, dreaming was a way of life. He dreamt so much of the time that the villagers began to talk.

"There goes that slow Appelemando,"
they called after him.

"He'll never amount to much."

"He never does anything useful."

"He dreams the day away."

Appelemando had four good and true friends.
"Don't listen to them," Jefftoe Fury said quietly.
"What do they know?" Lark Apostanoff snapped.

Petra and Dorma Opatoshoe cooed, "Besides, they don't know our secret, do they?"

It was certainly true. These five shared a very special secret, indeed.

Appelemando's dreams!

You see, whenever he daydreamed with his friends, they could actually SEE the dreams! Right out of the top of his head they drifted. They twisted through shafts of brilliant sunlight. Floated up, up, up into the sunny sky. There was so much to look at, animals, birds, flowers...all in wondrous, vibrant colors!

Appelemando enjoyed dreaming just for them.
He did big dreams.
He did tall dreams.
He did little dreams.
He did middle dreams.

One day, Lark announced, "Let's capture one of Appelemando's dreams on a piece of paper! Then we could look at it even when Appelemando isn't around!"

The children tried and tried to get the dreams to stay, but each time the dreams drifted off and disappeared. Then Petra and Dorma covered a piece of paper with water from the well tub they had been playing in. At that very instant, a dream floated up from Appelemando's head, and Lark and Jefftoe pushed the paper in front of it. It held fast.

"Hurray," they exclaimed for joy. "Now we can keep his dreams forever!"

It wasn't long before they discovered that Appelemando's dreams would stay on anything that was moist or damp.

Mops drying over balcony rails.

Laundry airing on clotheslines.

Bottoms of fat, white ducks waddling up the street.

"Boy, Appelemando," Jefftoe laughed, "you better not ever dream on a rainy day."

"What a mess we'd have," Lark snickered. "Lucky you only dream on sunny days!"

Then, one day when Appelemando had begun to dream, the sun suddenly hid behind gray storm clouds. The wind blustered, and rain dropped from the clouds above them.

"Oh no!" Lark squealed. "What are we going to do?"

"Appelemando, don't dream anymore," Jefftoe ordered.

"You just can't," Petra and Dorma said, as they were pelted with wet raindrops.

Lark clapped Appelemando's hat tight onto his head, but it was no use. The dream had already drifted up and was floating toward the buildings of the town.

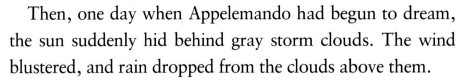

The children gasped as they watched each and every scene hold fast to the walls and storefronts of the town.

As soon as the rain stopped, the townsfolk came out of their houses and shops. They were stunned when they saw all of Appelemando's dreams on the walls.

"Someone has painted our houses and stores," a voice called out. "Who did this?" an angry woman cried. "I'll find who is responsible for this prank," the mayor said, as he saw the crowd that had gathered.

Then his eyes fell on the children. They were covered with Appelemando's dreams. "You!" the mayor shouted, as he started toward them. "What have you children done?"

The children were taken to the elders of the village.

"Do you mean to tell us that all of those things on our walls are dreams?" they asked when the children explained.

The more the children tried to tell the villagers about Appelemando's wonderful dreams, the more suspicious the elders became.

"If what you say is true, let's see Appelemando dream right now. Here in this place," the mayor snapped.

The elders leaned forward in their seats and watched Appelemando.

But the harder Appelemando tried to dream, the more impossible it became. Nothing at all would come into his mind.

Jefftoe, Lark, Petra, and Dorma all stared at the air above Appelemando's head waiting, waiting, but nothing appeared.

"I knew they were lying," a villager whispered.

"You should be ashamed of yourselves…such a ridiculous story," one elder said out loud.

"Let them scrub the walls," a voice rang out. "Fit punishment for painting our village without our permission!"

As the children walked toward home after the ordeal, they were afraid that Appelemando's wonderful dreams would never happen again. They walked and worried. In their sadness, they didn't watch the path. When they looked up, they were in the middle of the forest.

They had lost their way.

As hours passed, the children's families became more and more alarmed. They alerted all the people in the village, who sent out search parties to look for the children. "Where could they be?" they all pondered.

"Our people will never find us here," Petra and Dorma cried.

"They won't even know where to look," Jefftoe said sadly.

"If only we could signal them somehow," Lark said thoughtfully.

Then all of the children looked at Appelemando.

"You can help, Appelemando." Lark announced. "If you dream a dream big and bright enough, it will rise above the trees. People in the village will see it and know we are here."

"Yeah!" they all cheered.

But Appelemando was quiet. "I can't dream anymore," he cried.

"You have to try," they all said. "You must!"

All Appelemando could think of were the bitter words of the elders, the people who didn't believe him, and try as he might, nothing would appear in his mind. There was no dream.

Then he looked into the eyes of his friends. In Lark's eyes there was certainty. In Jefftoe's, steady sureness. In Petra's and Dorma's, complete expectation, for they loved his dreams.

Then he closed his eyes and began to see.

Bright colors of every hue, shape, and texture floated from
the top of Appelemando's head. They twisted through the air.
The wind caught them and lifted them above the trees.

Sure enough, the villagers saw the dream just above the forest where the children were. They all followed this vision and when they found the children, they wept for joy. Never again would they question the importance of dreams.

Now the village is no longer a drab place. The path leading to it is bustling with visitors drawn there by rich colors and soaring images that cover the walls of the town. Colorful scenes that its townsfolk are very proud of, indeed.

It is a dreamy place.

A wonderful place.

An old man sits by the fountain in the square. An old man who loves to dream. For him, dreams are magic chariots pulled through his mind by galloping hues of color. For him, dreaming is a way of life.